Dear Parent:

Congratulations! Your child is taking the first steps on an exciting journey. The destination? Independent reading!

STEP INTO READING® will help your child get there. The program offers five steps to reading success. Each step includes fun stories and colorful art. There are also Step into Reading Sticker Books, Step into Reading Math Readers, Step into Reading Write-In Readers, Step into Reading Phonics Readers, and Step into Reading Phonics First Steps! Boxed Sets—a complete literacy program with something for every child.

Learning to Read, Step by Step!

Ready to Read Preschool–Kindergarten
• big type and easy words • rhyme and rhythm • picture clues
For children who know the alphabet and are eager to begin reading.

Reading with Help Preschool–Grade 1
• basic vocabulary • short sentences • simple stories
For children who recognize familiar words and sound out new words with help.

Reading on Your Own Grades 1–3
• engaging characters • easy-to-follow plots • popular topics
For children who are ready to read on their own.

Reading Paragraphs Grades 2–3
• challenging vocabulary • short paragraphs • exciting stories
For newly independent readers who read simple sentences with confidence.

Ready for Chapters Grades 2–4
• chapters • longer paragraphs • full-color art
For children who want to take the plunge into chapter books but still like colorful pictures.

STEP INTO READING® is designed to give every child a successful reading experience. The grade levels are only guides. Children can progress through the steps at their own speed, developing confidence in their reading, no matter what their grade.

Remember, a lifetime love of reading starts with a single step!

Special thanks to Vicki Jaeger, Monica Okazaki, Rob Hudnut, Shelley Dvi-Vardhana, Jescya C. Durchin, Shea Wageman, Jennifer Twiner McCarron, Trevor Wyatt, Greg Richardson, Derek Goodfellow, Genevieve Lacombe, Theresa Johnston, Michael Douglas, David Pereira, Jonathon Busby, Sean Newton, Zoe Evamy, Steve Lumley, and Walter P. Martishius

www.stepintoreading.com
www.barbie.com

Educators and librarians, for a variety of teaching tools, visit us at
www.randomhouse.com/teachers

Library of Congress Cataloging-in-Publication Data
Redbank, Tennant.
Barbie in the 12 dancing princesses / adapted by Tennant Redbank ; based on the original screenplay by Cliff Ruby and Elana Lesser. — 1st ed.
p. cm. — (Step into reading. Step 2) "Barbie."
SUMMARY: This version of the fairy tale features Princess Genevieve and her eleven sisters as they escape their strict cousin by dancing the night away in a magic world, returning only to save their father, the king.
ISBN-13: 978-0-375-83780-7 (trade) — ISBN-13: 978-0-375-93780-4 (lib. bdg.)
ISBN-10: 0-375-83780-9 (trade) — ISBN-10: 0-375-93780-3 (lib. bdg.)
[1. Princesses. 2. Dancing. 3. Fairy tales. 4. Folklore—Germany.] I. Title: Barbie in the twelve dancing princesses. II. Title: 12 dancing princesses. III. Title: Twelve dancing princesses. IV. Grimm, Jacob, 1785–1863. V. Grimm, Wilhelm, 1786–1859. VI. Ruby, Cliff. VII. Lesser, Elana. VIII. Zertanzten Schuhe. English. IX. Title. X. Step into reading. Step 2 book.
PZ8.R247Bar 2006 398.2—dc22 2005035978

Printed in the United States of America

10 9 8 7 6 5 4 3 2 1

First Edition

STEP INTO READING® STEP 2

Adapted by Tennant Redbank

Based on the original screenplay
by Cliff Ruby & Elana Lesser

Random House New York

Princess Genevieve
and her eleven sisters
loved to dance.
They loved to be free.
Some people said
they did not behave.
So their father's cousin
came to help.
Her name was Rowena.

Rowena had a secret.
She wanted to be queen!

She made new rules
for the princesses.
No painting.
No singing.
Above all, no dancing!

The princesses
had new chores.
They had to clean
the garden.
They raked leaves.
It was hard work.

Then the king fell sick.
Rowena nursed him.
She made him tea.

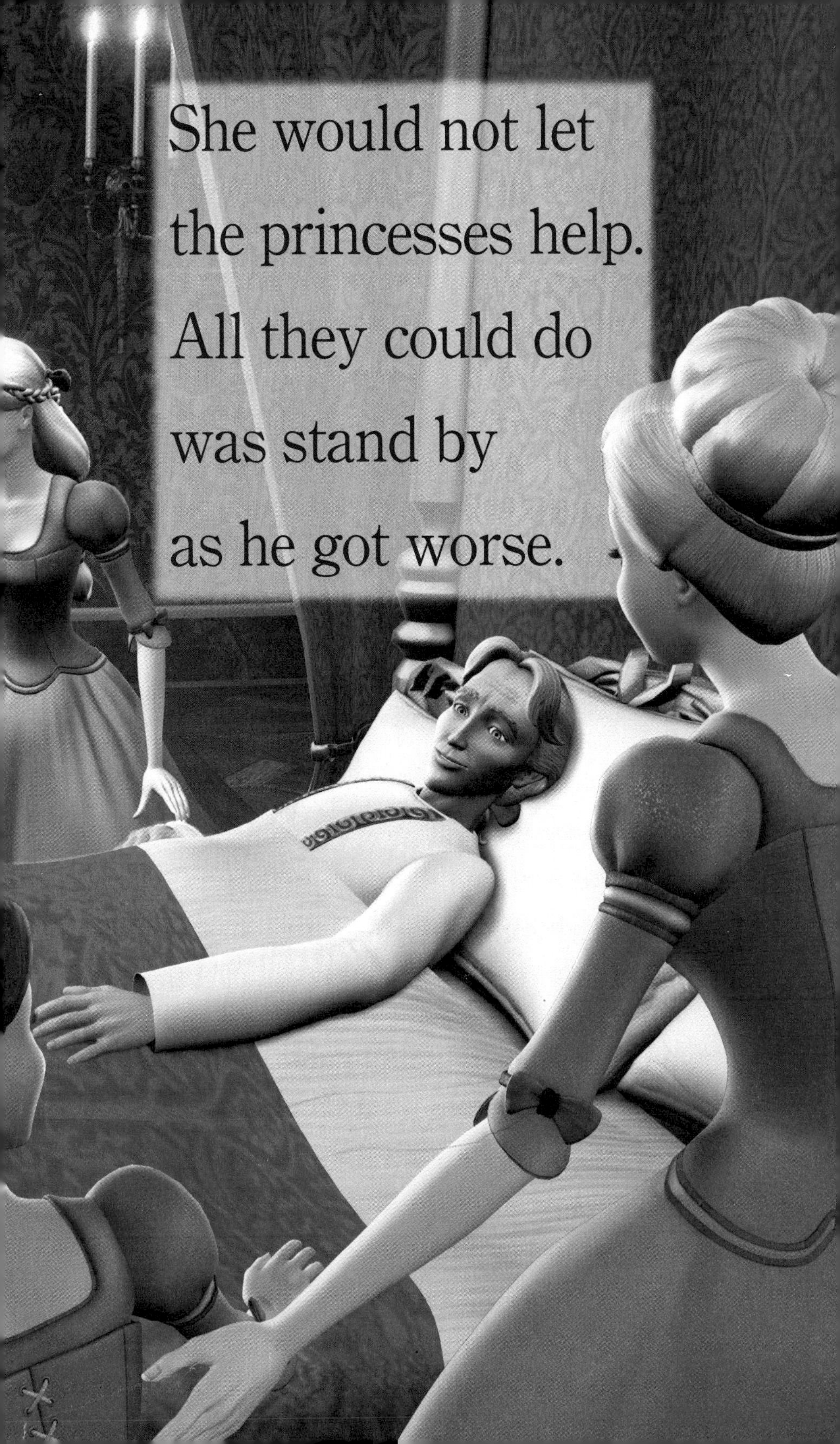

She would not let
the princesses help.
All they could do
was stand by
as he got worse.

The girls were sad.
In their room,
they dreamed
of the magic land
in their favorite book.

Just like in the story,
Genevieve leaped
from stone to stone.
Then she twirled.
The floor opened
to another world!

Gold and silver trees
stood around a lake.
Magic flowers
made wishes come true.
The princesses
danced and danced.
Lacey hurt her knee.
The lake's magic water
healed it right away!

In the morning,
their shoes
were worn out.
Derek, the shoemaker,
gave them new ones.

Genevieve danced
for him.
Step, step, twirl.

Rowena was angry.
She put a guard
outside their door.
She locked them in.
Yet the princesses
danced that night.

On the third night,
the spell would be over.
The girls had to choose
one place or the other.

Their father seemed
better off without them.
They decided to stay
in the magic world.

Derek had found out
Rowena's plan.
He wanted
to tell Genevieve.
He sneaked into
the girls' bedroom.
He saw footprints.
He stepped on them.
He twirled.
The floor opened.

Derek warned the sisters
about Rowena.
They had to go home!
But Rowena had found
the magic world.
She stole two flowers.
Then she trapped
the princesses!
Luckily, they found
another way out.

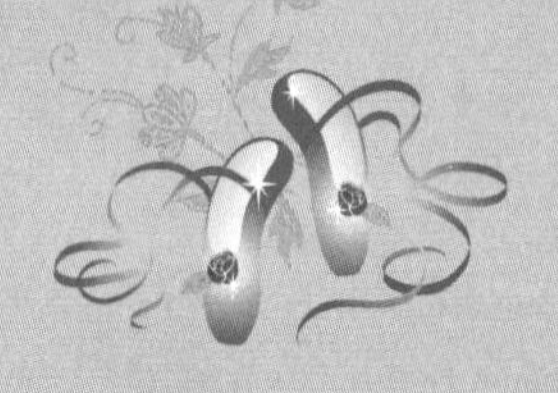

The king was very sick.
It was from Rowena's tea!
Derek and Genevieve
burst into his room.
Rowena used the dust
from one magic flower.
Two suits of armor
came to life!
They fought Derek.
But he won.

Rowena blew magic dust
at Genevieve.
"Dance your life away!"

Genevieve waved it away.
The dust fell on Rowena.
Her feet began to move.
She could not stop.

She danced
right out of the castle!

Lacey rushed
to her sick father.
She had magic water
from the lake.

She poured a few drops
in his mouth.
It worked!

Soon there was
a royal wedding . . .
for Genevieve and Derek,
princess and shoemaker.
Step, step, twirl.
They were a perfect fit!